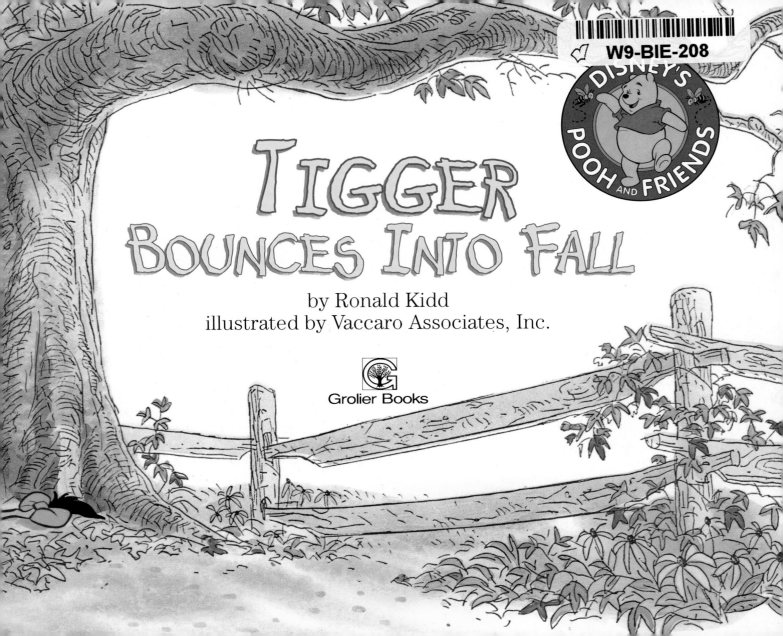

DISNEY'S
POOH AND FRIENDS

TIGGER BOUNCES INTO FALL

by Ronald Kidd

illustrated by Vaccaro Associates, Inc.

Grolier Books

Based on the Pooh stories by A.A. Milne [copyright the Pooh Properties Trust].

Edited by Ruth Lerner Perle
Produced by Graymont Enterprises, Inc.
Design and Art Direction by Michele Italiano-Perla
Pencil Layouts by Ennis McNulty
Painted by Lou Paleno

ISBN 0-7172-8447-6

Printed in the United States of America.

One day after summer had ended, Tigger was bouncing through the Hundred-Acre Wood. He bounced over stones and streams. He bounced past bushes and logs. He bounced just for the joy of bouncing, because that's what Tiggers do best.

As Tigger bounced, he heard a crunching sound. He looked down and saw that the ground was covered with leaves. Then he looked up and noticed that the tree branches above him were almost bare.

"Oh, no!" thought Tigger. "Something is making the leaves fall down!"

He bounced up and down, up and down, wondering what it could possibly be. Suddenly he thought he knew the answer.

Tigger stopped and stood very, very still.

3

Several days later, in another part of the forest, Winnie the Pooh was watching a leaf fall. It drifted from the top of the maple tree, past a scampering squirrel, down among the branches, until it came to rest on the tip of Pooh's nose.

Pooh crossed his eyes and studied the leaf, and he discovered a very surprising thing. He saw two leaves. Not only that, he saw two noses!

Most animals would be upset to learn that they had two noses. But Winnie the Pooh just smiled. For if he had two noses, he must also have two mouths.

Humming a happy hum, Pooh went to his cupboard and took out two jars of honey— one for each mouth. He brought them outside and set them down in front of him. As he dipped a paw into the first jar, Piglet came hurrying down the path.

"Pooh, come with me!" said Piglet. "Owl has called an important meeting!"

Pooh wondered what could be more important than honey, especially for a bear with two mouths. He couldn't think of anything, and so he licked the honey from his paw and said, "Piglet, would you care to join me in a little something?"

"Not now, Pooh. The others are waiting."

Pooh looked sadly at the honey jars and sighed. But then he got to his feet and followed Piglet.

Soon the two friends came to an open place where they found Owl, Kanga, Roo, Eeyore, and Rabbit. When Pooh and Piglet arrived, Owl stepped up onto a log and cleared his throat.

"It has come to my attention," said Owl, "that something is missing from the forest."

Pooh said, "Green."

"I beg your pardon?" said Owl.

"Green is missing from the forest," Pooh said. "Does anyone know where it went?"

Owl said, "I was thinking of something else. What's missing from the forest is...well, bouncing."

Owl was right. For the past few days, there had been no bounces at all. Where there were no bounces, there was no Tigger. And where there was no Tigger, there was no fun.

Roo cried, "Did Tigger go away?"

"I hope not," said Owl. "Why would he do that?"

Eeyore shifted from foot to foot...to foot to foot. Then he said in a sad voice, "I think I know why."

"Tell us," said Owl.

"Well," Eeyore began. "The last time I saw Tigger, he had made up a game called Bounce the House. And the house he decided to bounce was mine—not that my house is much to look at, but it is mine after all. So I told Tigger to go away and that's what he has done. He went away and it's all my fault."

"No, Eeyore, it's not your fault," Kanga said. "When he left your house, Tigger didn't go away. He came over to my house."

"He did?" said Eeyore.

"Yes. He picked up Roo and started to play Bounce the Baby. The bouncing got higher and higher. Finally I asked him to go play somewhere else. It's my fault that Tigger left us."

15

As Kanga spoke, Pooh noticed that Rabbit's ears had begun to droop. "Rabbit, is anything wrong?" asked Pooh.

"I'm afraid so," Rabbit said. "You see, Tigger didn't go away after leaving Kanga's house. He came to my garden and wanted to play Bounce the Carrots."

"Did you tell him to leave?" asked Owl.

"It's worse than that," Rabbit replied. "You know how he always says TTFN...ta-ta-for-now? I told him he should change it to TTFE."

"What does that stand for?" asked Piglet.

"Ta-ta-for-ever," said Rabbit.

16

A cold breeze blew through the forest.
"I miss Tigger," said Pooh.
"So do I!" Roo cried.
The others all agreed that they
missed Tigger, too.

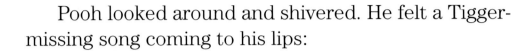

Pooh looked around and shivered. He felt a Tigger-missing song coming to his lips:

Oh, how I miss my bouncy friend.
I miss his giggles and TTFN.
I miss his noise while I'm trying to rest.
I miss his fun—that's what Tiggers do best.

I miss his happy. I miss his loud.
I miss his cheerful and eager and proud.
I miss his stripes that are orange and black.
I miss Tigger. I want him back.

Piglet said, "Maybe it's not too late to find Tigger. Let's go look for him!"

Everyone thought it was a fine idea. They searched all Tigger's favorite spots—the picnic rock, the sandy pit, and the floody place.

But Tigger was nowhere to be found.

Rabbit shook his head sadly. "It's my fault. And now Tigger is gone—forever."

21

Piglet, Eeyore, Kanga, Roo, and Pooh walked Rabbit home. On the way, Pooh pointed to some leafy trees and said, "Isn't that odd? I didn't know the forest had stripes."

"Stripes?" Piglet sniffled. "Please don't say that word, Pooh. It reminds me of Tigger."

"Hello there Pooh," said the stripes.

Pooh shook his head in amazement. "The forest has stripes, and it talks."

"So do Tiggers," said the stripes.

They peered in among the trees. There was Tigger!

Pooh called all the friends back together. It was a happy time, a thank-goodness time, a welcome-back time. And the happiest animal of all was Rabbit.

But something still wasn't right. Tigger seemed different. He seemed quiet and peaceful. They looked at him and tried to figure out what was wrong.

"I know what's wrong," Pooh said finally. "Tigger isn't bouncing."

It was true. Tigger was back, but he was standing perfectly still.

Owl said, "Tigger, you can bounce again. We promise not to be angry."

"I'm sorry I said ta-ta-forever," said Rabbit. "I didn't really mean it."

24

25

"That's not why I stopped bouncing," said Tigger. "I stopped because I was bouncing the leaves off the trees."

He picked up a handful of brown, crunchy leaves. "See? I knocked 'em off with my bouncing. It's all my fault!"

26

"Tigger," said Kanga, "have you ever heard of autumn?"
Tigger scratched his head. "Can't say I have," he said.
Kanga explained, "Autumn is the time of year when plants and animals get ready for winter. Chipmunks gather seeds. Squirrels hide in trees, and birds fly south."

"And bears store up their honey," said Pooh. "I think they might try a little taste first, just to make sure it's still good."

"Trees also get ready for winter," Kanga continued. "Every autumn most of their leaves turn yellow, orange, and red."

"Hey, I noticed that!" said Tigger.

Kanga added, "After turning colors, the leaves dry up and fall to the ground."

"Well, of course they do," said Tigger. "I bounced 'em there! And I promise, I won't ever, ever do it again."

"Oh, for goodness sake," Owl said, "you can't bounce leaves to the ground. They fall by themselves every autumn. It happened last year. Don't you remember?"

"It did," said Tigger, scratching his head.

"That's right," said Kanga. "And every spring new leaves grow back again."

"Really?" Tigger asked.

"Really," she said with a smile.

29

Tigger took a little hop. Then he jumped. Then he leaped. Then he bounced into the air.

"Hey, everybody, look at me!" Tigger cried. "I'm bouncin' again!"

And so he was. Tigger bounced over the bushes and through the leaves and back among his friends.

Once again, the Hundred-Acre Wood was a happy place to be.